For Mom,
who always encouraged me to ask questions

This book belongs to

Published by Roaring Brook Press
Roaring Brook Press is a division of Holtzbrinck Publishing Holdings Limited Partnership
120 Broadway, New York, NY 10271
mackids.com

Our books may be purchased in bulk for promotional, educational, or business use. Please contact your local bookseller or the Macmillan Corporate and Premium Sales Department at (800) 221-7945 ext. 5442 or by email at MacmillanSpecialMarkets@macmillan.com.

Library of Congress Control Number: 2022910192

First edition, 2023
Book design by Aram Kim

The artwork in this book was rendered digitally using Procreate and Adobe Photoshop.

Printed in China by Hung Hing Off-set Printing Co. Ltd., Heshan City, Guangdong Province

ISBN
978-1-250-83824-7
1 3 5 7 9 10
8 6 4 2

I HAVE A QUESTION

Andrew Arnold

Roaring Brook Press
New York

I look around the room, and nobody has a single question.

Nobody but *me*.

But I can't ask it, can I?
If I do, I know just what will happen.

I'll finally work up the courage
to raise my hand.

I'll ask my question, and everyone
will turn to me and laugh and say . . .

They'll most certainly give me a nickname.

But it won't matter, because
word travels fast these days.

I'll live there all by myself, where no one can make fun of me or call me names.

Finally, I'll be able to ask all the questions I want, any time I want.

NGH!

There will be just one small problem.

What good will that do?

I *have* to know.
I *have* to ask.

Okay, here we go.

Any moment now, someone will laugh or groan or roll their eyes.

Someone will most certainly call me Silly-Question Kid, because I should already know the answer.

But instead . . .

"What great questions, everyone!" says Ms. Gail.

"Before we answer them, are there any more?"